# A Lumen's Surrender

A DAEMONS & LUMENS NOVELLA

## S. D. PAINE

ISBN ebook: 979-8-9901373-8-7
ISBN Paperback: 979-8-9901373-9-4
Cover Design: Miblart
Editor: Andrea Halland, Editing by Andrea
Digital Formatting: Nicole Kincaid, Naughty Nook PR
Map Design: Amy @ tea_tomes_and_tropes

# DAEMONS & LUMENS SERIES

*Retaliation*

*A Daemon's Alliance*

*Resurrection*

*A Lumen's Surrender*

*Revolution*

*Memento vivre*
Remember to live.


Looking backward might be the only way to move forward.
-Taylor Swift


An ode to youth and the dreams we made.
To those who were forced out of childhood too soon.

# AUTHOR NOTE

This book contains dark themes and the characters make questionable decisions. Tropes and triggers include graphic violence, torture, and physical and mental assault.

For more information about this book and future books in the series, visit my website and sign up for my newsletter! www.sdpaineauthor.com

# NOVELLA PLAYLIST

*Find me on <u>Spotify</u> to listen to this Daemons & Lumens Playlist!*

Oh Death by Spiros May's & Bellabeth
Until I Found You by Stephen Sanchez
No Tears Left to Cry by Ariana Grande
Storm by Ruelle
Chasing Shadows by Alex Warren
Saved My Life by Sia
POV by Ariana
What Was I Made For by Billie Eilish
Ophelia by Lumineers
Just Keep Breathing by We the Kings
I Remember Everything by Zach Bryan and Kacey Musgraves
Legends by Kelsea Ballerini
Someone to You by Banners
Higher Ground by Odesza
Who Says by Selena Gomez
Saved My Life by Andy Grammar
Can't Be Tamed by Miley Cyrus
Wake Me Up by Avicii
Depressed in Heaven by Davvn
As the World Caves In by Sarah Cothran
Bruises by Renee Rapp
Cruel World by Active Child
Waves by Dotan
End of Beginning by DJO

We Are Broken by Paramore

Save You a Seat by Alex Warren

Back to Life by Hailey Steinfield

Lunch by Billie Eilish

Wannabe by Spice Girls

# THE V.I.P. LIST

Seraphina Valdis Bronwen - Daughter of Aurora Valdis

Aurora Valdis Bronwen - Mother of Lailah, Seraphina, and Michaela, Deceased

Joseph Bronwen - Husband of Aurora Valdis, Father of Michaela, Deceased

Lailah Valdis Bronwen - Oldest daughter of Aurora Valdis, sacrificed, Deceased

Michaela Valdis Bronwen - Youngest daughter of Aurora and Joseph

Nuriela Ramas - Lumen, mate of Lailah Valdis

Laszlo Blackbyrn - King of The Obscuritas, Leader

Darren Radnor - King of The Obscuritas, Enforcer, Deceased

Samuel Delano - King of The Obscuritas, Seducer

Ezekiel Parrish - King of The Obscuritas, Technician, Deceased

King Corson Ormaenus - King of Caligo and all daemons

Prince Belial Ormaenus - Oldest son, Prince of Caligo and loyal to the king

Prince Morax "Mor" Ormaenus - Middle son, Prince of Caligo

Prince Phenex "Phen" Ormaenus - Youngest son, Prince of Caligo

## PAWNS & PLAYERS

Belfegor - Daemon, King of the Novo Mountain Tribe, deceased

Adriel Uthra - Father of Lailah Valdis, family is part of the Lumen Council, deceased

Gremory Cerravaux - Daemon, Commander of the Daemon Army

Delphine Bellinor - Powerful witch, of The Mal-Regia
Foras - Daemon soldier

The Malefica - Akin to witches, living in Tellisa
The Mal-Regia - Royals of The Malefica

# IMPORTANT PLACES

Stella Terra (Stel-uh Tare-uh) - Planet of the daemons and lumens

Tellisa (Teh-lee-sah) - Country of the daemons and lumens

Caligo (Cal-ee-go) - Capital city of the daemons territory

Caelum (Kay-lum) - Capital city of the lumens territory

Calesia (Kuh-LEE-zia) - City near the mountains where the witches reside

Dariava Palace (Dar-ee-ahvah) - Home of the Valdis family, rulers of Caelum

Zamina Castle (Zah-me-nuh) - Home of the Ormaenus family, rulers of Caligo

Mount Monkara (Mahn-kaw-rah) - Protected mountain home of the truxen daemons

# OBSCURITAS

The Obcuritas - Exclusive cult seeking otherworldly power

Daemons - Monstrous creatures of myths and legends, varying degrees of magic/power relating to the elements, prone to power over earth and fire

Lumens - Ethereal creatures of myths and legends, varying degrees of magic/power relating to the elements, prone to power over water and air

stellatium (stuh-lay-tea-um) - Rare metal created from a dying star, powerful enough to kill a daemon or lumen

luxenite (lux-eh-night) - Rare stone, magically charged to harness the power of a lumen's essence tenebrite (teh-neh-bright) - Rare stone, magically charged to harness the power of a daemon's essence

Vis-el (Veez-elle) - Elemental power of the daemons and lumens, different from the spells wielded by The Malefica

truxen daemon - Type of daemon with the ability to shift into any creature and communicate with animals, very rare

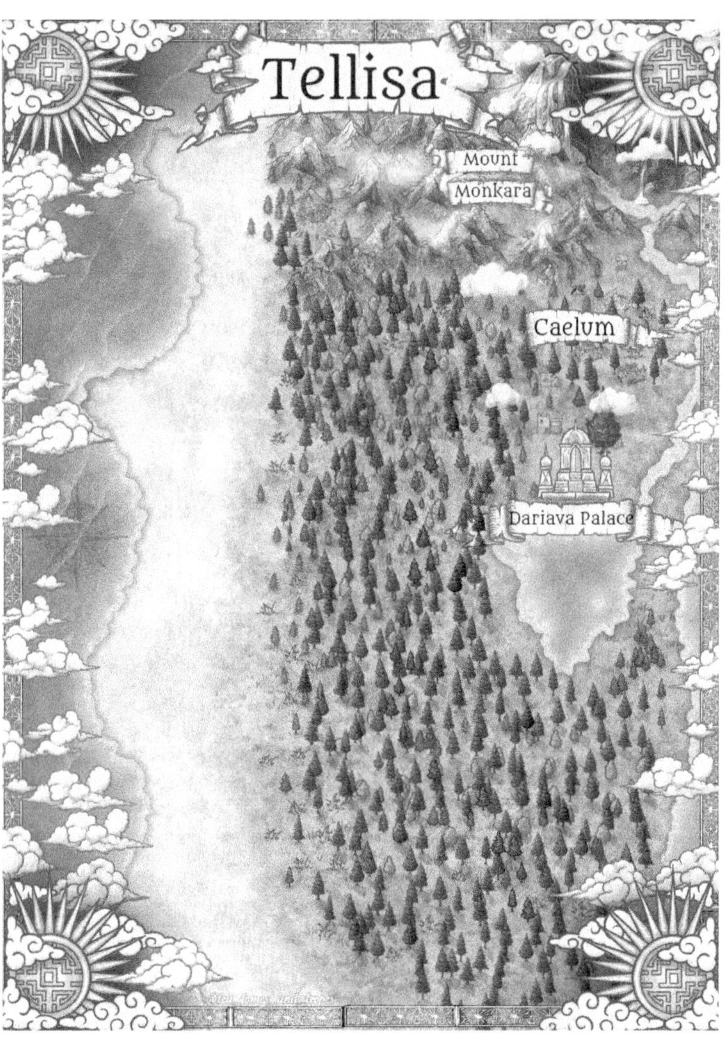

Tellisa
Mount Monkara
Caelum
Dariava Palace

# PROLOGUE

## Aurora

The visions were causing pain unlike anything I had ever felt. It was my own fault for ignoring them for as long as I did. Lately, my dreams foretold something terrible was coming. I could taste my own death. The stars whispered of fates unfolding and new powers emerging, and not all of them were good.

Lailah's soft giggle pulled me back to reality, only for the visions to shift once more, burrowing into my mind like an avalanche and forcing me to witness her death. A sob escaped before I could stop it, and my little toddler turned her bright eyes to me.

"Momma!" she cried out, her arms raised and face full of concern.

My knees hit the marble floor of the palace as the visions grew in intensity. Belfegor swooped into the room moments later, sensing my distress through our bond.

"What is it?" He spoke softly, scooping Lailah into his muscular arms and rushing to my side in one swift motion. His knees brushed against my own where he knelt. "What can I do?"

Death and destruction filled my head. I brought my hands up, pulling my golden hair and squeezing my brain to ease the pain. "The end. It's coming for them. My babies."

Belfegor's hand snapped out, a possessive growl escaping his lips as he gently brushed over the baby growing within my belly. "No one will harm my girls. I will burn the world to ash if they try."

Tears stung my eyes as I looked up at this brave daemon of mine. "I know you would, my love. But you won't be here to do so. Neither of us will."

Belfegor's eyes clouded in anguish, his face a mirror of my own heartbreak. He squeezed Lailah tightly in his arms and kissed her forehead. "Then we will do everything in our power to set them on the path to victory. Our daughters will be as brave and strong as their mother. And when they defeat the great evil you've seen, we will watch them proudly from the stars. Together."

I nodded. There was more truth to his words now than he knew. Belfegor's power gave him insight to the future, even when he didn't realize it. Seraphina, his fierce daughter, would be so like him. It broke my heart that they wouldn't know each other.

"Yes." I stood slowly, and my protective mate wrapped his free arm around my waist. "There is much to do, and not enough time to do it. It is not only our world that will be affected by the coming war."

Belfegor leaned down and kissed my forehead, his bright-green eyes shining with a love so brazen it took my breath away. "I am yours to command, queen of my heart."

Power pulsed in my veins, and a vision came forth, offering the smallest glimpse of a future where my children were safe. The vision was fleeting and plagued by countless others with terrible outcomes. I leaned into my mate and the unending strength he offered within the circle of his arms. Before our deaths, we would secure that future of happiness for our girls.

Upon my life and the stars above, I willed it to be so.

# CHAPTER ONE

## Lailah

The wind whipped through my hair, whisps flying across my eyes and blocking my vision as I ran for the sea. The call of the ocean was stronger now that my powers had awakened. I laughed, whispering to the winds to push me faster to my destination. Nuri shouted behind me, attempting to snatch my dress and pull me back, but I was one with the wind in this moment. I sucked in a breath, licking the salty air brushing across my lips.

We raced through the trees toward the beach. Dariava Palace was surrounded by dense forests but still relatively close to the sea. It was our favorite place to go. This particular beach was more remote and heavily guarded for the royal family's use. There were some perks to being a princess, at least.

"I'm going to catch you!" Nuri shouted behind me, and I grinned.

"The sea is mine!" I taunted her, leaping over a fallen tree and slamming my feet into the soft white sand. My wings itched to unfurl, but that would be cheating.

The rules were only minimal powers while we raced and no transformations. I coaxed the winds to keep my feet steady and fill my lungs with enough oxygen to outrun my best friend.

Nuri and I were competitive from the start, but in the best way. She was my favorite being in the entire world. More than my sisters, for sure. We had a connection I couldn't explain, at least not until I turned sixteen and our powers truly emerged. Daemons and lumens were born with affinities to the elements, but our abilities to manipulate them fully manifested at the Vis-El Ceremony, the rite of passage for every creature. When the stars blessed Nuri and I at the ceremony, our powers awoke and a thread of purest gold unfurled within me, connecting directly to her.

I never told her about it. The force of it was intimidating. My mother, of course, asked if I had any bonds forming after the ceremony. She always had that sly smile when she spoke about Nuri. Aurora Valdis was the greatest Seer in all of Stella Terra. Her power was renowned throughout the clans of witches, daemons, and lumens. There were whispers it was a power I would inherit, but I didn't want anything to do with it.

When I gained access to the Vis-El, our power, and the visions didn't come forth like they had for her, I was beyond relieved. No super serious future duties for me. Well, almost. But my mother handled that disaster of a situation, and now here I was. Free of royal betrothals and ready to explore the world with Nuri at my side.

Waves crashed against the shore, drowning my thoughts and bringing me back to the competition at hand. One I was clearly going to win.

"Victory is mine!" I shouted, leaping into the air and ready to feel the ocean before us. But just as I leapt, the waves whooshed out to sea and nothing but sand remained beneath my feet.

"Not today!" Nuri shouted, rushing by me and diving into the sea, using her affinity for water to call the ocean to her instead.

Her dark hair disappeared beneath the waves, and I growled in frustration, kicking the sand. Nuri's head popped up, and seconds later, a massive wave crashed over me, pulling me out to sea. Air wrapped around my head, allowing me to breathe under the water.

I spotted Nuri's silvery blue eyes flashing underwater and dove toward her. Where I was fair-haired and golden eyed, Nuriela was dark-haired and had shining silver eyes. She was my starry night, and I was her rising sun. Nuri reached for me, and when our hands clasped, power zipped between us. I shivered under the water at the feel of it. We swam together, reaching the surface with bubbling laughs.

The ocean was clearest blue and green, going on for miles around us. Being in the water was almost as cozy as being in the sky.

"You win." I grinned, splashing her while we treaded water.

"I know," she teased, letting go of my hand to float on her back. "The sea will always choose me. Just like the winds will always help you."

My body floated next to hers, and we stared up at the bright-blue sky. Puffy white clouds drifted above us, and I ached to join them. While I could manipulate water almost as well as Nuriela, she was right. My connection to air was stronger.

"For now," I teased. "My control over the sea is growing."

"And so is my connection to the sky," she taunted, smirking back at me.

"Let's make a bet. By my next name day, I bet my powers are stronger than yours."

Nuri laughed, and the sound stirred butterflies within my stomach. "Not a chance. I'm already stronger. In a years' time, I'll be twice as badass as I am now. I'll take your bet."

She wasn't wrong. Nuri was crazy powerful. But I was a Valdis and more than confident my powers would, at the least, match hers. The first year after the ceremony was the most important. Our connections to the elements and the magic pulsing in every living expounded over time. Some lesser daemons or lumens didn't gain any further power or bonds after their awakening. But I wouldn't be one of those.

My eyes dropped to her lips, perfectly pink and heart-shaped. "Deal."

She cocked her head, gazing at me inquisitively. But I wasn't quite ready to cross that line. It was stupid, really. I knew she was meant for me, and I for her. Whether it was written in the stars for us to be fated mates or not, my heart belonged to Nuriela, now and always. And yet I hesitated. It wasn't like we never touched, but those touches were innocent. Friendly. I longed for more, dreamt of it every night.

But how does one go from having a best friend to a girlfriend?

# CHAPTER TWO

## Lailah

Nuriela swam closer to me and reached out, brushing her fingers against my arms. Our legs bumped beneath us as we treaded water. "What are you thinking?"

Her silver eyes pulsed with light, and my power surged in return, the golden light shining for her and only her. "I'm thinking about…how glad I am that my mother ended the arrangement."

Nuri scowled. "As if you could ever marry that daemon. He's vile." Her skin pulsed with silver light, and the seas rocked around us as her anger grew. "I can't believe your father set that shit up."

I sighed, my shoulders slumping in the water. "I can."

Things with my father were complicated. Less now, since he died. I didn't really get to know him, because his life was snuffed out when I was only a handful of years old. Every girl wants to know her father, and I was desperate to remember mine. But my mother never spoke of him. She was forced to marry him in an arrangement with another important family. While the Valdis family was the most powerful, the Uthras were nearly as strong. My father, Adriel Uthra, was the eldest son and supposedly one of the most talented lumens in our history. His mastery of the elements was known throughout our people. It was said he could even steal power from daemons. How, I wasn't sure.

When I told Nuri about him and how I wanted to know more, she immediately snuck into the Angea Library. It housed every bit of lumen history and a few things on the daemons, witches, and other creatures, too. Knowledge was power, my mother always said, but in the wrong hands, it was the end of all things. She was sort of dramatic sometimes.

Within the dusty scrolls of the most powerful families, we found everything about my father's campaigns in battle. His unyielding will led the lumens to victory over the daemons thousands of years ago. He was a conquering hero, and when the Uthras came to the palace to pledge their loyalty to the Valdis royal family, Adriel saw my mother and claimed her for his wife.

They were together for hundreds of years before I was finally born. I never had the courage to ask her how or why she didn't have more children in all those years. But when she met Seraphina's father and my sister came screaming into this world soon after, my suspicions grew.

Adriel Uthra was not a good male. One night, Nuri and I concocted a truth serum and dosed a few of the generals in the lumen army who knew him best. We stole the recipe from a witch's grimoire hidden deep in the library. The spelled males told us of my father's strength, but also his terrible cruelty. We fled the tavern, my emotions spiraling at all I had heard.

A few years before my powers were awakened, the general of the daemon army arrived at the palace gates. His name was Gremory, and the gossips of the palace claimed he was quite handsome for a daemon. He flirted with every single lumen as he made his way through the palace, or so I heard. Mother forbade me to be in the throne room when he arrived. He presented her with a contract, signed in blood by my father, promising me to the eldest son of Corson Ormaenus. His name was Belial. Nuri and I of course looked up all tellings of this stupid prince and found what I expected—he was just as terrible as my father.

When my powers were awakened and The Sight did not come as it had for my mother, the relief I felt was infinite. I was just another lumen; royal yes, but Belial wanted a powerful tool to wield, not just a wife. Or so I hoped. The daemons were persistent, and Gremory returned each week to remind my mother of the contract. Each week, she begged off with one excuse or another, until there was nothing left to do but refuse.

And she did.

Gremory did not return after she finally rejected the proposal. I wasn't sure what that meant, but it couldn't be good. We found that out soon enough when Seraphina's father was murdered by lumen traitors and daemons colluding to bring down our family. He was a force of nature, and without him and his powerful clan of truxen daemons, my mother was vulnerable. We were vulnerable. The last women of the Valdis line. A male heir hadn't been produced in centuries.

Since Belfegor's death, my mother grew more and more withdrawn. She closed the palace to all lumens except those she trusted completely. Her only happiness, besides Sara and I, came from the human, Joseph, and my youngest sister, who was half-human.

I couldn't understand how my mother could fall in love with a human, especially when she'd had a daemon like Belfegor. It was also strange to me how he could allow her to be with Joseph too. My mother's love life was seriously a mystery. And not one I cared for the details of. She didn't say much about it, other than when Seraphina asked if our mother still "loved her papa" after Michaela was born and we realized Joseph was her father, not Belfegor.

Belfegor had responded first. He scooped Seraphina up in his arms, and she giggled, snatching his beard in her hands. "Your mother's heart has room for us all, little princess. Joseph is a good male. He will care for you, even when I cannot."

Belfegor's response was odd, but I didn't think much of it at the time. Reflecting on it now, perhaps Sara's father knew he wouldn't be around long enough to see his daughter grow up.

After his death, my mother took my sisters to stay with Joseph more and more. She forced me to tag along on a few trips to their world. Michaela's father wasn't so terrible, but he was sort of dull and completely powerless. Mother said staying with the humans was a good thing, that we could hide from those who would harm us in our world by staying there. But I hated that place. Stella Terra was my home, and I would never agree to leave this world of magical creatures. I didn't care how dangerous it was to stay.

All these heavy thoughts were ruining the good mood this day started with. Floating in the clear blue water, my body felt weighed down by burdens I didn't want. I shook my head in frustration. My wings ached to come out as anger clouded my thoughts, and I leapt into the air. Nuri followed me, her pale-blue wings snapping out as she chased me through the clouds.

I pushed my own wings to go faster, darting through the sky and letting out a scream of frustration.

Nuri suddenly collided with me in the air, wrapping her body around my own. My skin heated at the connection.

"What's wrong?" Nuri gripped my face, forcing me to look at her. "The air is thick with your sadness. What are you keeping from me?"

I closed my eyes, unable to keep this secret any longer. "My mother says we are leaving. We're going to Earth. Permanently. She's taking Kaela and Sara there tonight. And by the end of the week, we'll be gone."

Nuriela's face fell, a helpless look in her beautiful eyes. "Then I'll come with you."

My body shook with hopeless anger. "I've already begged. She refuses. She said it's not safe for anyone to be with us right now."

"I don't fucking care!" Nuri snarled, her nails digging into my face, and I relished the pain. "We are meant to be together, Lailah. Forever. Nothing is going to keep us apart."

Nuri's fierce gaze pierced my soul, and I knew she spoke the truth.

"Let's run away. Right now. We'll go to the mountains. Or cross the sea and create an island of our own to call home. I don't care about being a princess or my mother or any of it. I just want you."

She smiled at me, and my gaze fell to her perfect mouth once more. My skin flushed as I registered the heat building throughout my body, barely clothed and pressed to hers as our wings flapped in the breeze, keeping us aloft in the sky.

Nuri was my everything. The most beautiful being I had ever known, inside and out. All I needed was her. In this life and all the others. Only her.

"Let's do it." Nuri leaned in and pressed her lips to mine.

Power zipped through my body the moment it happened, and I almost moaned at the heady feeling of it. I kissed her back, threading my fingers in her hair. Her soft lips parted slightly, and I mimicked the action, tasting the sea on her breath. It didn't last long and our movements were a little rocky, but it was our first kiss. And I would cherish the memory of it forever.

# CHAPTER THREE

## Nuriela

We were finally breaking free of our chains. Lailah and I weren't meant for this life of royal rules and arranged marriages. From the moment we met, a piece of my heart became hers. And little pieces continued to break away until my entire soul belonged to Lailah Valdis. She was so incredibly strong, so talented, and made for more than the life of a princess.

The news of her mother's plans to leave nearly crushed me. But hope renewed when Lailah suggested we run away together. And of course I agreed, because I would do anything for her. Even so, a tiny voice in the back of my head lagged, like a warning that the path I was on wasn't quite right.

The voice was my grandmother's. Not literally, but it was my grandmother who had this talent. For me, it presented as more of a sixth sense warning of danger. I wasn't nearly as powerful as her, but she always said I had a bit of witch magic in me, and at the right moment, it would emerge. My family came from a long line of lumens, until my grandfather fell in love with a witch. He broke generations of traditions. And while it wasn't outlawed then, it was still rare for creatures to mix. She was the one and only witch in our family. I never got to meet her family, the other witches. Perhaps now it was time. Lailah and I could travel to Calesia, the hidden city of the Mal-Regia. My grandmother was a member of their royal family. Maybe if I used my connection, they would help us. It was worth a shot. Being left behind while Lailah and her family fled to Earth was not an option.

Lailah and I spent the afternoon sunning on the beach, enjoying the quiet afternoon and reveling in our last day in Caelum. I would miss this city, but a life without my mate wasn't a life at all.

I knew Lailah was meant to be mine from the moment I met her. And when my power awakened, a thread of brightest silver unfurled within me, leading directly to my mate. Of course, we weren't truly mated yet. Daemons and lumens could often find their mates in youth, but the connection didn't fully take root until we turned nineteen. While our power awakened at sixteen, it needed time to evolve. When that happened, I knew with every fiber of my being that we would be mated.

When the sun began to set, Lailah and I walked back to the palace. Aurora was taking Seraphina and Michaela away, and it would be our best chance to escape without her Seer powers catching us.

While I wasn't as confident we could outwit the greatest Seer of all time, Lailah was certain this plan would work. Aurora would be focused on Joseph and Lailah's sisters. One of the many mysteries of Lailah's mother was her connection to a human male, and then a halfling daughter. It made sense for Michaela to be in the human world. With so little power, she'd be snuffed out in an instant in Caelum, and especially in Caligo. I didn't see how taking Seraphina and Lailah away from their home was the right decision, though. Yes, there was growing unrest among the lumens, and probably more drama than the adults shared with us, but we were strong. Aurora had allies, she just needed to use them.

My thoughts were growing too dark, and the woods were suddenly eerily quiet. Tension rolled off Lailah in waves moments before she cried out.

Lailah doubled over and held her head, her face scrunched in agony. "Nuri. Something is wrong."

I dropped to the forest floor and caressed her cheek, hating the pain written in her features. "What is it?"

Lailah shook her head. "I don't know. I think someone is coming and—"

"Hello, princess," a voice whispered from the shadows of the trees.

I whipped around, ready to defend. "Who's there? Show yourself." I snarled, trying to sound brave even as my heart pounded erratically.

The deep voice growled. "You do not command me, sordida. I've come to claim what is mine."

The use of that word was a slap in the face. Dirty. Unclean. It was used for creatures like me, with impure family lineage. And only the biggest assholes uttered it.

"Belial," I growled the name. The wind picked up, and I felt Lailah's panic from her position crouched behind me. "You can't have her."

The monster stepped out from the trees, along with a dozen more daemons. We were severely outnumbered. He was massive. His tanned skin glowed with a ghostly light, and his eyes shined crimson red. His dark horns and midnight-black wings matched his black heart. There was no love in his eyes. Not even lust. All I could see was greed. He would take Lailah from me and use her up until my mate withered and died. It was written plainly on his face, and he didn't even try to hide it.

"Nuri," Lailah whispered, her voice hoarse. "Run. Please, go."

Absolutely not. I snarled at her, gripping her chin and forcing her to look at me. "Never. Be free, Lailah. I love you."

Her eyes widened, but there was no time for Lailah to stop me. In the next second, I whipped around and sent a tidal wave toward the daemons. While Belial spoke, I was calling to the sea, gathering the ocean and bringing it here. The waves crashed into the daemons, and several of them cried out as they were swept away. Belial turned to shield himself, and it was the window I needed to save her.

Turning back to my mate, I used every ounce of air magic I could muster and lifted her above the trees. I begged the wind to carry her back to the palace. Lailah screamed at me, the sound of her voice fading as she was carried into the clouds.

My lungs burned with the need for oxygen, and my limbs grew heavy. The amount of power I used in those two actions drained me completely. But my grandmother raised a warrior, and my mate was safe. I squared my shoulders and faced the snarling daemons rushing toward me. If my death bought Lailah's life, I'd welcome the darkness with open arms.

# CHAPTER FOUR

## Lailah

Tears flowed down my cheeks as Nuri's magic dropped me directly in front of two very stunned guards at the palace gates. They recovered quickly and alerted everyone in the palace of daemons nearby. Our army was always ready, and lumens mobilized quickly, taking to the woods. I prayed they would reach Nuriela in time.

Belial came for me, but instead Nuri sacrificed herself. My heart was breaking into a million pieces, and only seeing her alive and well would put it back together. My skull felt like it was splitting in half, another reason why I was unable to stop Nuri. I couldn't focus, could barely run, stumbling through the palace and shouting for my mother.

*I'm coming, daughter. Meet me in my rooms.*

My mother's voice rang out in my mind, and I ran as fast as I could through the halls. When I reached her room, I shoved the doors open. They slammed into the walls, and I glanced around, searching for her. Aurora shimmered into existence in the middle of the room, and I leapt into her arms.

"I'm here, Lailah. It's alright," she soothed, but I was beyond that.

"It's most definitely not alright, mother!" I shouted at her. "Belial is here in Caelum. He came for me. Nuri caught them off guard, and now she's there in the woods with him, drained and alone. Please help her!"

Aurora Valdis was mysterious to most, her emotions always guarded and hidden from prying eyes. But in this moment, she looked down at me with so much love and sorrow that my heart ached. "He's taken her, my love. But she isn't dead."

I shoved away from her angrily. "I know that. I would feel it if she were dead. But he's going to hurt her. He will kill her, mother."

"And if you go to her now, he will take you, too." Aurora's voice was that of a queen. A queen with too many burdens bearing down on her shoulders.

But I didn't care about any of that. "I would rather die at her side than live any kind of life without her. Tell me how I can save her. I know you've seen it."

My mother shook her head. "I haven't. But you can."

Her words stopped me. "What do you mean? I don't have The Sight. You know this."

She smiled at me. "Oh, my love. Do you truly believe that?"

I swallowed, my blood rushing through my body with guilt and shame. How could she know? How could she know I had a vision just moments ago? The force of it blasted through my mind, and I almost passed out before we were attacked. It showed me Nuri's death. Her painful, horrible death. And my own.

"I can't, mother. Please don't make me." The words rushing out of me sounded pathetic. But I didn't want the visions. Couldn't stomach seeing her hurting like that.

Aurora strode toward me, graceful as always. Her soft hands brushed my tear-stained cheeks. "I cannot make you. It is your burden and your gift. Accept it, let it in."

My shoulders fell, and I shook my head. "I'm scared."

"As was I, when I was your age. Fear still lives within me every day, Lailah. But I don't let it rule me. Let the visions flow through you and use them to create new paths. You can save her." Her voice shook with emotion, and I let her words seep into my skin and take root.

If I let the visions in, I could use them to save Nuriela. But then the other one would come back, too. The one where I was laid out, my wings destroyed, and men chanted foreign words. As soon as that vision came, I knew it was my true death, could taste the reality of it on my tongue.

And yet, what I saw in those visions didn't matter. If my death meant life for Nuri, then I would accept that fate. I would surrender to my power. Closing my eyes, I opened the door within my mind that was locking away that part of my power. A flood of strange magic crashed through my veins. Dozens of visions played out before my eyes. Flashes of places and faces I didn't recognize. There was death and destruction, but there was life, too. I saw my sisters falling in love, their bonds to each other stronger than ever. And Nuri. She was there. She looked fierce as hell and stunning.

Fresh tears flooded my eyes. Because she was there in my visions, alive and safe, but it wasn't me at her side.

"Focus, Lailah." My mother's voice reached me through the haze of visions. "Focus on Nuriela."

That was easy. My thoughts were always of her. I saw Belial, his plans, his strange army. His only desire was power. My power. And I would bring it to him willingly.

# CHAPTER FIVE

## Nuriela

Screams of agony tore through the silence, pulling me from the dark. They were likely other prisoners of Belial's, which meant I was in some kind of dungeon. My head throbbed, and every muscle in my body ached. The evil prince's daemons beat me with claws and hooves. Even my elevated healing abilities couldn't work fast enough to take away the pain of their rage. At some point in their brutality, I passed out. And now I was locked in a cage inside a dark room. It was small, barely tall enough for me to stand. I gripped the bars to pull myself up, hissing in pain. It burned like frostbite against my skin. The metal was stellatium, one of the only things in this world that could truly hurt daemons or lumens.

Pain lanced my side, and I lifted my shirt to see an open slash, blood still weeping from the wound. It must have been a stellatium blade. I closed my eyes and willed my body to heal itself. The flesh stitched itself over slowly, stealing most of my strength, leaving a tiny white line scar across my abdomen. A mark I would bear until my passing. These assholes would pay for that. The room I was caged in was cold and bare. Small window slits high up on the walls let in early evening light. No guards stood within the room, but likely a few were posted outside the doors.

This was most definitely a trap. I should be dead, but instead I was Belial's path to Lailah. If I wasn't such a coward, I'd take my own life now and set her free of the burden of rescuing me. But I just couldn't. Our life together was supposed to be at the beginning, not the end. And it was too soon to give up hope. Perhaps if I could find a way out of this cage, my power would return enough for me to escape. The stupid stellatium pulsed around me like a second heartbeat, keeping me weak.

The door opened with a loud clang, and two guards stepped into the room, followed by the monster who kidnapped me.

"Belial." I spat his name as if it were an ugly thing, because it was. He was.

The daemon didn't even flinch, although his jaw ticked subtly. This male didn't take kindly to those who weren't whimpering in subservience. Well, too bad for him, I wasn't the type to bow—unless Lailah was asking.

"Nuriela Ramas," he purred, the sound something out of nightmares. I resisted the urge to shiver in revulsion. "I had hoped to bring Lailah here, but this is just as well. Better, even. With you here, she is likely to obey my every command more willingly."

"Doubtful," I snarled at him.

Belial smirked. "The mate bond is impossibly strong between you already, even without consummation. I am most certain when she sees you in pain, bleeding before me, she will break."

I slammed into the bars, ignoring the pain. "You know nothing of our bond. Or her strength. She will not be yours, now or ever."

My words rang out with authority, but inside, my blood sizzled with anxious fear. The shining bond tying me to Lailah pulsed with life, and I knew she would come for me, just as I would for her. Hopefully when she did, I'd be out of this stupid cage and fighting at her side.

"We shall see, lumen trash." Belial's eyes burned with rage, but his voice shook with a hint of uncertainty.

I grinned, enjoying his unease at my defiant words. And maybe that was a mistake. The last thing I saw before the darkness claimed me was a large clawed daemon fist coming at my face.

Hours passed, and I was still locked in the stellatium cage. My power was a meager flicker within my soul, but at least my body no longer throbbed from the beating I received earlier. When the doors of the room opened, I crouched on the balls of my feet, ready to fight, but instead of daemons, a single human male walked into the room.

"Who are you?" I questioned, curious and more than a little suspicious. There weren't many humans on Stella Terra. Only the witches took them in. To daemons, they were slaves and to lumens, they were nothing. Lailah and I heard horror stories of the awful things daemons did to humans. Humans were a weakness, in my opinion, and they didn't belong in our world.

But this one, he had an aura about him. There was power in his blood. Not like daemons or lumens, but witches.

"I am Ezekiel." The man spoke softly, weaving his hands in a strange pattern before spreading his fingers wide and sending a pulse of his magic into the air.

The magic cloaked my skin like a film. It didn't hurt, but I remained vigilant. His softness could be a trick.

"We can speak plainly now," he continued. "I've used a spell to muffle the sound in the room."

Ezekiel walked closer to the cage as he spoke. He was tall for a human, several inches above my 5'7" height. His skin was tanned, and his dark hair was swept away from his face in a "I'm a mess but trying to keep it together" sort of way. His dark eyes remained locked on my own. He wore a black cloak with a symbol I didn't recognize resting over his left breast.

"What do you want?" I asked him, preferring to be direct and get this over and done with. "Are you here to help me?"

He nodded but frowned. "I am, but not in the way you think. You will escape this place, Lailah will be here soon to save you."

My heart beat ten times faster at his words, and hope blossomed within me. "This doesn't sound like bad news."

Ezekiel wrung his hands through his cloak, crinkling it, clearly anxious. "It will take most of Aurora's power to keep Belial in this world when she flees to mine. Her power cannot be wasted in aiding you now. Listen closely."

His words were like half-truths and riddles I didn't fully understand, but I memorized them all. Ezekiel came closer and spoke a few words to open the cage before stepping back.

"Take the hall all the way down and go left. Run as quickly as you can and try not to be loud about it." Ezekiel's words were frantic, his movements agitated. "Find Lailah and get back to Aurora immediately."

I nodded, perfectly fine with that plan. "We will."

# CHAPTER SIX

## Lailah

Nuri was somewhere below ground level. Her soul called to mine, and even without the full power of our mate bond, I could sense her. My feet stumbled over each other as visions plowed through my mind like flashes of a movie. They were chaotic and hardly made sense. My mother said I needed to focus on certain people to help guide the visions, so I filled my thoughts with Nuri.

The problem with doing so was that in all the visions with her in them, I was gone. Something was coming, and whatever that disaster was, it would separate us. But what was it? If I could see it, maybe I could find a way around that fate.

The thought of being parted from her was not just a punch to the gut, it was like my heart was being wrenched in half. *How could I live with only half a heart?*

Caligo's royal castle was heavily guarded, but one of my visions showed me sneaking in through a window at the top of a turret on the east side. Among the stones were barely visible handholds, made by someone decades ago. The stone was smooth from years of use. Just the thought of it brought on another vision. A daemon prince sneaking out of the castle. This one was different, his face was filled with mischief, not greed like his older brother.

I climbed the stones quickly, choosing not to fly in case someone spotted my bright-white wings. The moment I hopped onto the window ledge, I froze. The visions did *not* show me the prince would be waiting in his room on my arrival.

He was already an imposing figure, despite his young age. He couldn't be more than a hundred years old, which was young for a daemon. Daemons and lumens aged differently than humans. It took creatures like us decades to age up to a quarter century. The first sixteen years flew by similar to humans, but once our powers emerged, the aging process slowed significantly. And then after the age of twenty-five, it could be a millennia before our flesh began to show any signs of aging.

"Hello, Lailah, is it?" The prince smirked, twirling a ball of fire in one hand.

I stiffened. "How do you know me?"

"Well, my elder brother has been raging about the princess who eluded him, and the lumen he captured instead as bait." The prince tossed the fire back and forth between his hands absentmindedly.

"Of course she's being used as bait." I rolled my eyes, but kept my power at the ready. "And yet there weren't many guards. Certainly none as I climbed into this room."

The prince smirked, silver eyes glowing with power. "I suppose he thinks no one in this castle would dare make a move against his wishes."

My power tingled beneath my flesh, ready to be unleashed. "But you would?"

The prince grinned, flashing his sharpened canines. "Yes, I would. We met once, you know. You were an infant then. I'm Phenex, the best looking prince of the three of us."

As soon as he spoke his name, visions flared to life within my mind. A beautiful blue-haired girl appeared, familiar and foreign all at once. Seraphina. She was with this prince, fighting at his side. And there was something more.

"You met Belfegor before he died." I whispered, straightening out of my fighting stance.

Phenex went rigid, his playful fire snuffed out. "What did you say?"

I sighed, more visions coming as my thoughts remained tied to the prince. "Remember his words. Don't give up. Don't give up on her. She will need you in the darkest hour."

Phenex nodded grimly, his eyes darkening. "I will never give up on my mate."

It seemed I could trust this daemon prince. "Good. Now take me to mine."

We raced through the castle at speed, Phenex leading the way. A roar of anger filled my heart with fear. Someone pissed off Belial, and I had one guess who that person was. My Nuri was too fierce for her own good, and I refused to let these assholes hurt her because of me.

Phenex stopped short, just before a set of massive wood and iron doors. He turned to me with that trickster grin. "I'll go in first."

He didn't give me time to respond before pushing open the doors and sauntering into the room. I jumped to the side so Belial wouldn't see me.

"Bels, what's this about? I never pegged you for a sub," Phenex taunted his brutish brother, feigning a nonchalant attitude.

I chanced a glance through the doorway, and my heart lurched at the sight of Nuriela straddling Belial, a block of ice encasing his head and his hands. The daemon's fire attempted to melt her icy cage, but Nuri, my badass best friend, held her own.

"Nuri!" I shouted, unable to wait any longer, but it was a mistake. As soon as I shouted, her focus turned to me and Belial's fire power rushed out in a fury of flames.

Nuri jumped back, her wings snapping out to lift her up and out of the flames engulfing the prince. I raced for her, but a wall of fire appeared between us.

Belial snarled. "I was going to offer your petulant mate a quicker death, but now I plan to have you both watch while I torture the other."

"You will never touch her again!" Fury laced each of my words with venom I didn't even know I had. The thought of this monster hurting Nuri made my blood boil, and power thrummed through my body. I closed my eyes, calling on The Sight to guide me.

The reason he craved this power, the reason all daemons and lumens, and even witches, revered it, was not only because it allowed you to to see all things past, present and future, but also manipulate the very fabric of time. I might be new to its strength, but the movements and words I needed flowed through me as if they were always there.

"I command you, STOP!" I brought my hands together in a clap that rebounded off the walls as loud as two cymbals crashing.

Belial's movements slowed, and his fire stalled and stuttered. Nuri rushed through the smoke and landed at my side.

"We need to find the King." Worry filled Nuri's voice. "King Corson. Belial, he bound my power to the King, and we need to kill him."

More visions flooded my mind, and I shook my head. "No. If we don't leave now, we will both die."

Nuri's face fell. "But how can I stay connected to that monster? He's as bad as Belial. They say he's even worse, the things he does to women, to their slaves."

Another vision flared up, and I scrunched my face in confusion. "I don't think that's right. There's something dark in his mind, something not his own." I couldn't make out exactly what was happening, and we didn't have time to linger. "Remember Lo. She's the key. Now run."

Nuri turned and fled for the window, opening it and readying to jump. She stopped, waiting for me, but I had one more thing to do first.

I stalked closer to Belial, my power pulsing with life. I smirked at the silent roar stuck on his stupid face. A bright aura cloaked my skin as I let The Sight take hold of me in this moment. When I spoke next, my voice was not one, but many, echoing through the room. Phenex's eyes widened, the only movement he could make in his frozen state.

"I have seen your death, Belial. And even though I won't be around to witness your end, I take heart in knowing my sisters will be the ones to get revenge. And trust me when I say I will do everything in my power to bring that fate to you and yours."

# CHAPTER SEVEN

## Nuriela

I didn't speak as we flew high in the clouds, away from the daemon city. My thoughts were a mess of anger and fear. The implication of what Lailah had said to Belial was clear. She wasn't going to survive this. Whatever this mess was, she and I would not be coming out of it together.

The thought nearly had me smashing face first into the dirt when we landed outside the palace.

"Are you alright?" Lailah asked softly, catching my elbow.

Her touch sent a zip of feeling straight to my toes. But even that couldn't sway my feelings right now. "Why did you tell him you wouldn't be around to see his death?"

Lailah's face fell, her shoulders slumping as if the weight of all the worlds rested on them. "Because I won't be. I've seen it."

"No," I snapped, the refusal cold and flat. "No, Lailah. We said we were going to leave all this behind. What about us?"

Tears filled her eyes, and pain pierced my heart for making it happen. "I will never forget about us. Even in this, I'm putting you first. Knowing you will survive this gives me the strength to do what I need to do. And I need you with me when the time comes."

Her words sounded foreign. Her voice changed. This was not the same girl I held in the ocean only days ago. Lailah was becoming a fierce woman, a queen. How could I refuse her?

The answer was simple, I couldn't.

I took her soft hand in mine and dropped down to one knee, staring up into the eyes of the only woman I would ever love. "Lailah, my queen, my best friend, my mate. You've had my heart since birth, and when you go, so too will a piece of my soul. I am yours to command, Princess of Caelum."

Lailah's shining blue eyes filled with fresh tears, and her bright-blonde hair twisted in the breeze. She was the most beautiful creature in the world.

She brought her free hand down and brushed her fingers against my cheek. I leaned into her touch. "I love you, too, Nuri. I wish we had time for the adventures. But this is the only way for us to win the war to come. I surrender to this fate, just as you surrender to me. Just know, my heart is yours. It's always been yours."

Her words broke me, filled me with love and devastation all at once. But I would not fail her. Not now, not ever. "What do we do now?"

Lailah pulled me to my feet and gripped both my hands. "We go to Earth. You aren't supposed to come with us, but every vision I see shows you practically ripping the fabric of time apart because you refuse to be left behind."

I snorted a laugh. "Sounds about right."

She grinned, and for a moment, we were two young lumens with nothing but adventures before us. "Once we get to Earth, there won't be much time before the cult leaders come for us.

You must stay out of sight, no matter what. They cannot find you, Nuri. What comes next will be important, and only you can save her."

"Save who?" I searched her eyes feverishly, absorbing every word she spoke.

"I don't know her. But when you find her, you will know she is the one who needs saving." Lailah's voice held an eerie echo, as if other voices were connected with hers in that moment.

The seriousness of her tone told me all I needed to know. "I will find her. I promise."

# CHAPTER EIGHT

## Lailah

My mother waited for us within the castle, ready to whisk us away to a new world. Nuriela had never been to Earth before, and the shock of going from a world with endless power to one with suppressed magic would be jarring. It was for me, the first time. I also had a speech ready to beg my mother to allow Nuri to come, but she simply smiled and grabbed both our hands.

The Sight came so easily to her, of course, with so many years of practice. For me it was a kaleidoscope of faces, places and emotions. Trying to focus was a near impossible task, but when I let the power flow through me without forcing it, like my mother suggested, it was easier.

I was not prepared for the sight that greeted me when we got to Earth. My sisters were suddenly several years older. I was frozen to the floor when Seraphina came bouncing into the living room of Joseph's house and leapt into my arms several years older than the last time I saw her. Michaela followed her, only a couple years younger by the looks of her. My eyeballs nearly jumped out of their sockets.

After they went to bed, my mother sat us down on the couch, her eyes soft. She masked her emotions well, but I could see her exhaustion in the slump of her shoulders.

"Thank you, my love," Aurora murmured as Joseph placed a steaming cup of tea in front of her.

He returned to the kitchen and came back with two hot chocolates for Nuriela and I. It was early spring here, and a cool breeze blew through the house.

Joseph lived in the state of Michigan, close to some massive body of water I couldn't remember the name of. The last time I visited, it was late summer and my sisters and I ran amok between the rows and rows of cherry trees. It was quite beautiful here, for something created entirely without magic.

Aurora cleared her throat, pulling me from my memories. "I know it's strange, and I will ask forgiveness for stealing away some of their childhood, but their minds won't remember the loss. Not for some time."

"But you had to?" I asked, sipping the creamy hot cocoa.

Aurora nodded, and Joseph squeezed her hand. Her bright-blue eyes were clouded with emotions I was still too young to fully understand. "Yes. Belial is in league with a cult called The Obscuritas. And while you might think humans are weaker than us, they are no less dangerous. The Kings of this cult have acquired immeasurable power."

"And we can't defeat them?" Nuri cut in, fierce as ever.

Aurora sighed. "No, we cannot. Our world is divided, and there are not enough of us to win this battle. The Kings will come for Lailah and I in two  nights. They will take us all, except you, Nuriela."

I nodded. "I saw that, too. She can't be with us."

Nuri's gaze snapped to mine. I could tell she wanted to protest, but I squeezed her hand, silently begging her to trust me. The vision of her death at the hands of this cult was too much. As long as she stayed away, it wouldn't come to pass.

Joseph, having been silent while my mother laid out the plan, reached over and squeezed my arm. His wolf-like brown eyes caught mine. "Thank you, Lailah."

My eyes drifted to my mother and back. I was unsure what he meant. "For what?"

"This is only possible because of you. Our worlds will have a chance to survive this, because of you. Thank you. Thank you for giving Michaela that chance."

My eyes welled with emotion, and a vision of Michaela and Seraphina laughing together passed through my mind. "I would do anything for her. For my family."

"As would I." He nodded, a darkness passing over his eyes. "As will we all, before the end."

The conversation ended on a heavier note, and my body felt like it weighed a million pounds. The heaviness in my heart was difficult to bear.

"Hey." Nuri interrupted my dark thoughts, threading my arm through hers. "Let's go for a walk."

I smiled up at her. She was a whole two inches taller. "That sounds nice."

We left the house and wandered toward the cliffs overlooking the tumultuous waters below. The sky was overcast, rain threatening to spoil our walk, but we continued on in silence. Nuri paused as the nearly full moon peaked out from the clouds. She dropped to the grass and pulled me down beside her. We lay there, staring up at the dark sky. Her slim fingers brushed against my palm. Heat pooled within me at her gentle touch. I closed my eyes and let this moment imprint on my mind.

Nuri turned her head toward mine. "What do you think we would have been, if we lived to be a century old? Where would we be?" she whispered, her lips mere centimeters from my ear. The warmth of her breath tingled against my neck.

My eyes opened slowly, and I rolled onto my side, facing her, never letting go of her hand. "We would be the most fearsome warriors. Our combined power would be nearly unmatched. We'd roam the worlds, seeking out adventures, taking out bad guys and making a name for ourselves throughout the galaxies."

Nuri smiled. "Yes. And we'd be mated. Finally bound and eternally together."

Her lips nearly brushed mine as she spoke. The thread of light leading me to her pulsed with love and sweet desire. Warmth flooded my limbs, and I leaned in, pressing my lips firmly to hers. Nuri's soft lips parted, and I tasted the fire within her. Her desire matched my own in every way.

She pulled away first, our breaths heavy and gazes hooded with need for the other. Our love was a bright, brilliant thing, never to fully be unleashed. "I will find you in the stars, Lailah Valdis."

"Vi et animo." I spoke the words of our people. The words two lovers spoke when declaring themselves to each other in a formal ceremony. This wasn't formal, and no contract or consummated bond held us, but I felt it all the same.

"Vi et animo," Nuri whispered back, leaning in and kissing me lightly. She flinched at the exact moment I did, tiny splashes hitting our cheeks.

We turned in unison as the sky opened up and rain fell from the clouds. Either one of us could've used power to keep us dry, keep the rain away. But neither of us did. Our bond pulsed with life, and I sucked in a breath. Nuri wanted to feel fully alive and in this moment as much as I did. Her fierce love washed through me as the mate bond solidified. In my soul, I could feel our threads of silver and gold braiding together. This was unheard of, a mate bond forming when we were both so young and newly awakened.

Nuri squeezed my hand, her chest heaving. "Do you feel it?"

I squeezed hers in return. "I feel you."

We smiled at each other, our hearts filled with awe and a love so brilliant and pure. It was everything I knew it would be. We lay there in silence, feeling this new connection and reveling in this moment of happiness the stars blessed us with.

I embraced the rain, begging the element my mate connected with most to wash away my fears and doubts, leaving only my love for Nuriela behind. The summer storm melted the last of my stubborn refusal of this fate and let it sink away into the earth.

"I surrender," I whispered to the stars, letting them know I was ready. I could do this. For my family. For my mate.

# CHAPTER NINE

## Nuriela

Strange scents filled the air as I walked with the Valdis family into what Lailah called a "county fair." She said small towns held these little festivals filled with games, food, and these terribly dangerous looking rides. Our people brought the mortals many things over the centuries, but this was something they invented all on their own. We had no need for such things when we could fly. Their bodies were so fragile, and yet they took risks.

It was curious, but then I suppose we all took risks to feel something.

I slipped my hand into Lailah's, threading our fingers together. She didn't turn, but I swelled with pride at the flush of her cheeks and small smile on her lips.

No one knew us here, and before all the bad things coming to us truly began, I wanted her to feel happiness.

"I want to ride that one!" Seraphina shouted, pointing at a ride of some kind made entirely of rusted metal. Of course, she would choose the one that looked the most dangerous.

A boy about the same age as Lailah and I seemed to zero in on Seraphina when she giggled with delight as she eyed the death trap of a ride. He stood out to me. His clothes were plain, and his movements were nonchalant, but there was something off about him, like he didn't belong.

Aurora laughed at her middle child's giddy behavior, her own smile bright and infectious, drawing my attention away from the boy. Lailah's laugh was so similar to her mother's, and I loved being the one to bring it out of her.

"What do you want to do, Lailah?" I squeezed her hand, gesturing to the death ride. "I know it's not that."

She laughed. "I don't have the death wish my sister does. Let's get a funnel cake. I want to see your face when you try it."

Joseph handed Lailah some form of currency, and she pulled me into a jog away from the others. I trailed behind her, holding her hand tightly. My blood zipped with adrenaline that only she could provide. Her wavy blonde hair bounced down her back, and I resisted the urge to run my fingers through it. Lailah turned back to me, a carefree look about her that I'd never seen before. It lit me up from the inside out, my soul completely intune with hers.

She stopped at a stand to order this funnel cake, and the smell was, I had to admit, mouthwatering. Lailah paid for the food, and we found an empty table to sit and enjoy the treat. I straddled the bench, facing her, and waited as she ripped a tiny piece of the cake-like food.

"Open," she commanded with a cheeky grin.

"Since when are you in charge?" I smirked at her but opened my mouth.

Lailah reached out slowly and placed the cake onto my tongue. Her soft fingers brushed against my lips, and I stopped myself from licking them. My stomach curled with something more magical than butterflies, and the bond between us pulsed with need.

Sugary goodness exploded in my mouth, and an involuntary moan escaped my lips. Lailah's eyes snapped to my mouth, and the flush of her cheeks matched the heat in my own.

"Do you like it?" she whispered, her pink tongue flicking out to lick her bottom lip.

I brushed my thumb over my mouth, powdered sugar coating it. Before I could second-guess my actions, I pressed my thumb to her plump lips. She opened for me, and I nearly lit on fire when she sucked my thumb into her mouth.

"It's delicious," I murmured, my voice rough. Her eyes snapped to mine just as I pulled my thumb back and gave it a slow lick, tasting her. "Almost as sweet as you."

Lailah's bright-blue eyes filled with tears. "I wish we had more time."

This wouldn't do. I shook my head fiercely. "None of that. Tonight we live fully. Save your tears for another day."

If there was anything I could do for her, it was this. She needed to laugh, to feel joy. The weight of the world rested on her shoulders, and it killed me that I couldn't take away her burden. So if all I could give her was this night, then it would be the best one she ever had.

# CHAPTER TEN

## Aurora

We lay in our bed, limbs entangled after hours of lovemaking. Joseph worshipped every inch of my flesh, whispering his praises, memorizing the sounds I made when his lips caressed my skin. And I did the same, needing to feel the power of his love before our world was utterly broken. We only had hours until the Kings arrived. The visions were subdued while we enjoyed each other, but they were coming back with a vengeance. I could control them, for the most part. Decades of practice made it easier to push them into separate corners of my mind. Past, present, and future each had a room within my mind. The door to the past I opened often, searching for clues among the actions of our ancestors to assist my children and ensure their future successes. The door to the future I spent too much time behind. But how could I not, knowing the future had no place for me in it. And the door to the present, it was the one I spent the least amount of time with. My grandmother would scold me for avoiding part of my gift, but living in those visions was more heartbreaking than the others. My daughters would grow up without their mother, or their fathers, and I hated The Sight for showing me that fate.

A dull ache spread in my heart as I thought of the men I loved. Lailah's father was not among them. He was a duty, forced upon me by the Lumen Council and the fact that I was the last female heir of the Valdis line. My Seer gifts were already thriving by the time Adriel was presented to me, and I saw his vile thoughts. He was a manipulator. Charming and handsome on the outside, dark and cruel on the inside. He would take and take from me until I was nothing more than a husk of the woman I once was. But he was mine, nonetheless.

When the first vision of my beautiful girl Lailah came to me, I fled to the mountains. In those days, although daemons and lumens weren't friendly, we weren't in open war. The truxen daemons controlled the mountains and never showed themselves to what they saw as the lessers.

Truxens held a connection to creatures that even the royal libraries had no knowledge of. And they kept their strange powers hidden deep within Mount Monkara. But for whatever reason, at least none that I knew at the time, I always felt safe there, as if someone was watching over me.

And he was. My mate.

I remembered that day as clearly as if it were just hours ago.

*The soft soil was wet with my tears. My nails dug into the earth, anger and fear flooding my veins and making my power pulse out at a steady beat.*

*"Young queen, the animals are growing agitated by your cries,"* *a deep voice murmured from the shadows. Night had fallen, and only a sliver of moonlight offered little light. "What can I do to make you smile? A face like yours I imagine looks most radiant when you smile."*

*His words made me pause, and while part of me wanted to roll my eyes, another was grateful for the distraction from my impending marriage bed.*

*"Can you give me a new life? Because the one I've been dealt is terrible," I grumbled, still feeling miserable.*

*The shadows stirred, and the daemon slipped gracefully from behind a massive pine tree. He was nearly as broad as the trunk. His horns were a deep brown, earthy and rough like the bark of the very trees we stood between. His wings were forest green and scaled like a dragon, shimmering with gold whenever he walked beneath the moon's light. He was shirtless, his toned muscles very much on display. But even in all his masculine glory, it was his eyes that drew me in. They were the brightest shade of green, and my own ocean-blue gaze was instantly lost in his.*

*The moment our eyes connected, a soft moan left my lips. He inhaled, his pupils dilating and his fangs snapping out. My sorrow spiraled, mixed with a new devastation. This strange and glorious daemon was my mate. I could feel it in my blood as my power pulsed with new life in his presence.*

*Our silence lasted for many minutes as we assessed each other and accepted this knowledge. He moved with the grace of a jungle cat and the confidence of the falcon. His eyes, flecked with gold, shone with wonder and a possessive light. He dropped to his knees before me and lifted his massive hands to take one of my own.*

*"My lady." His deep voice shook with emotions I couldn't fully understand. "I have dreamt of you, of this day. My mate would bring the beginning of a new age."*

*My eyes were as round as saucers. "I...I am promised to another."*

*The daemon snarled. "No. Show him to me and I will kill him."*

*A surprised laugh escaped my lips, and he cocked his head, staring at me. "I'm not against that idea. But I must marry him. I will bear his child. My firstborn daughter will be the one who sets the future of our people on the right path."*

*My voice changed as I spoke those final words, the vision of Lailah clear in my mind.*

*The daemon stood, still holding my small hands in his. "If you must endure this burden, so will I. Marry this lesser male and do what must be done. Then I will end him. I will raise his child as my own. I am Belfegor of the Gaelicho Clan, and this is my vow to you."*

"Which door are you lost behind, my love?" Joseph whispered, caressing my cheek. His quiet words brought me back to the present.

"The past. My first encounter with Belfegor."

Joseph continued to caress my cheek, his thumb brushing across my bottom lip and making blood rush to my face at his touch. "It was one of those moments when the universe aligned just right. He was always there when you needed him."

I nodded, a single tear rolling down my cheek. "I wish it was different. That I could have kept you both. What a fierce family we could have made, all together."

Joseph chuckled softly. "Belfy. I do miss him. Even though his sexual appetite nearly killed me."

I moaned at his words, remembering the one and only time Joseph and Belfegor worshipped my body together. It was the most magical night of my life, right behind the births of my three fierce daughters. Belfegor was not only possessive of me, he owned Joseph, too. I shivered, and my husband wrapped his arms around my waist, pulling me closer until I could feel his hard cock pressed into my stomach.

"Close your eyes, my love," Joseph ordered. "Think of him while I make you come. Let us remember that night once more, before the end."

His hand dipped between my thighs, and I cried out when he teased me with his fingers. Tears streaked my face, sorrow and purest happiness warring within me for the men I loved and the life we would never have together.

Wrapping my arms around his neck, I kissed Joseph with all the love I had. My power pulsed with need, and my skin began to glow as his body joined with mine. He whispered filthy things, his voice dropping lower to resemble our mate, our Belfegor.

On this last night of my life, I sent my soul to the stars and begged for them to watch over those I loved most.

# CHAPTER ELEVEN

## Lailah

I woke up in a cold sweat, fear gripping my heart so tightly I was afraid it would shatter into pieces. My breaths came in quick gasps as my panic rose. The Obscuritas were coming. They were almost here. Dozens of visions plagued my mind. If Nuri and I tried to run, they would find us and kill her. I screamed as her throat was slit right in front of me. Another vision of Joseph trying to run for it with Michaela flashed in my mind. He was gunned down, and Michaela became their captive. Every path we tried led to the deaths of everyone we loved. Only in our capture would we survive. Or at least, some of us would.

My mother swept silently into the room. She knelt gracefully beside my bed and brushed her fingers through my hair. Her power pulsed gently, and a cool breeze caressed my damp skin.

"My darling first born," Aurora whispered, her eyes shining with love. "I'm so sorry this is the fate you were given. I wanted so much more for you. For all of you. I would give my own life to change it."

"It wouldn't matter," I sighed, wiping a tear from my cheek. "If you died now, we'd all die, too. I've seen it."

Aurora nodded, continuing to run her slender fingers through my hair. "I've seen it, too."

Her presence soothed my soul, and I felt a new sort of awe for my mother and her ability to remain strong in the face of all this. "How did you live with the visions of our deaths for so long? It feels like my heart is breaking with each one."

Her eyes shuttered. "It took many years to compartmentalize. And I wish I had more time to teach you."

Guilt bubbled out of me. "I wish my power emerged sooner. Maybe if I hadn't been so afraid of it, the power would've awoken within me and I could save them and—"

"Hush, my love." My mother shook her head. "Your power arrived precisely when it was meant to." Her head suddenly snapped to the door, and I knew it was time.

"They're coming," I whispered. She nodded, holding my face in her hands, and I willed myself to be as brave as she looked in that moment. "This will work, won't it, mother? I can save them all?"

Tears filled her bright aqua eyes, so like Seraphina's, and she smiled down at me. "Yes, my beauty. You have the power to set the course for your sisters."

I nodded, strength growing within me as well as my faith in my abilities to make this happen. "Hopefully Seraphina doesn't get in her own way. She is so ridiculous, sometimes."

Aurora chuckled softly, and it warmed my heart that I could make her smile. "She is so like her father."

The mention of Belfegor made us both frown.

"I wish you didn't have to be in so much pain, mother."

Her soft smile returned. Aurora pulled me from my bed, and I stood before her. She was tall, and even now, her shoulders were squared and proud. "Only in death is there room for rebirth."

Power pulsed around us at her words, and the vision of Seraphina's triumph flashed brightly in my mind. I grinned. "And what a resurrection it will be."

Aurora grinned back at me, my brave and powerful mother. "I love you, Lailah, my beautiful girl. My soul. Let's give them a little hell before we surrender, shall we?"

My mother held out her hand, and I took it, feeling the wind thrashing in my veins, begging to be unleashed. We might be the ones taken captive this night, but there was no vision saying we couldn't take a few creepy cult soldiers down with us before the end.

# CHAPTER TWELVE

## Nuriela

The Obscuritas came in the dead of night. I lay low, using my power to keep hidden high up in an oak tree in the front yard of the house. The pulse of Lailah's fear as she was dragged out of the house nearly sent me into a rage. But I couldn't ruin this, not when Lailah asked me to trust her. And I did, completely.

There were also several daemons and a couple lumens in the service of this cult. I noted their faces, memorizing them for later. Because there would come a time when I was strong enough to fight, and every one of them would be on my list.

Aurora stormed out of the house, her wings snapping out and glowing like starlight. She roared at the vile creatures who came for her family. It was too much to hope that this would be a happy ending, that she would take them all out right here and now.

I strained my heightened sense of hearing to catch her words, but there was something blocking me out. Lailah punched the daemon holding her hostage, and I smirked. He let go, and she returned to her mother's side. The pair spoke to the enemies for a few more moments then went back into the house.

Minutes later, the three SUVs pulled out onto the road with the Valdis family following them in their own vehicle. I waited a few minutes before following. The assholes probably warded the shit out of those vehicles and anything close to them.

My wings unfurled, and I leapt into the air, trailing them while keeping the clouds wrapped around me and out of sight. The drive was short, leading to a private airplane hangar where Lailah and her family were forced onto a plane.

Now that my power was fully restored, I was ready for this. Yes, I would stay out of sight, but there was absolutely no way I would be left behind. If I had to fly across the entire country in one night, so be it. This Earth wasn't entirely unfamiliar. Lailah had told me stories of the places they traveled to and what the people were like. I knew enough, at least, to blend in when I needed to.

The wind came to my aid, and I used its powerful gusts to increase my speed. The small plane flew for about four hours, and the ache in my wings settled when I finally landed on the roof of the sprawling mansion below. Not quite as big or nearly as beautiful as the Dariava Palace, but more dark and moody. I rolled my eyes, probably what these idiots thought daemons liked. They had no idea.

Lailah's golden hair shone even in the night, and I tracked her path into the mansion before taking flight, searching for a way in. There were several turrets with windows, and I spotted one that was slightly ajar. Slipping into the tower, I crouched on the wood floor and listened for the sound of footsteps. None came, and I released a breath. The ritual would begin when the full moon rose to its highest, brightest spot in the sky.

Everything in me screamed to intervene and take Lailah away. But I promised her I wouldn't. She was going to die, and I had to sit here and let it happen. Had anyone ever sat idly by and watched as the love of their entire being was killed? I suppose Joseph was doing so. He might understand the pain. At least two of his daughters would still be here to keep him from his despair. Lailah said I was strong enough to handle this, but as the little pieces of my heart that belonged to her began to blacken, I wasn't so sure she was right. I would never love another. And no one could make me think otherwise.

Chanting echoed up through the estate. The ritual had begun. With the cult assholes now occupied, I crept down from the tower and through the house, needing to be closer to Lailah in her final moments.

My blood heated, and bile threatened to spill from my lips. It took every ounce of my control not to save her like my soul screamed for me to do. Lailah's scream pierced the air, and I doubled over, feeling her pain. But there was no fear. In this moment of agony, she was not afraid. My brave, powerful Lailah. If she could do this, so could I.

# CHAPTER THIRTEEN

## Lailah

I thought dying would hurt, but it was the humiliation that caused me actual pain. They dressed me in a simple white dress, the fabric so thin I knew my body was on display. The hooded figures reached out as I passed through the circle, touching me, pinching my skin and pulling my hair. I swallowed my fear and continued on. The Kings waited for me. My family was still locked in cells on the lower level, for now. My mother said she would come, though, before the end, and that they would be safe, free. Until that time, I was on my own.

The guard behind me shoved me to the floor, and I winced as my knees slammed into the marble. My wrists were chained in front of me, and a cloaked figure attached the cuffs to a heavy chain embedded in the floor. One of the Kings came forward. I knew instantly who he was, having seen him, and how he would hurt my sisters, in my visions. He was massive, a monster of a human with evil lurking in his eyes. He crouched down in front of me, cocking his head.

"You're a pretty one." Dark intent laced his deep voice. "If only I had more time, we could have had real fun together."

The King reached into his pocket and pulled out a small blade. He flicked the blade open and swiftly cut down the center of my dress, revealing my breasts. He traced the blade along my bare skin, flicking my nipple with the sharp edge. I remained still, frozen and willing my body not to react. He wanted my fear, but I would not give in.

He chuckled. "Yes, it would have been a real treat to break you. But don't worry, I'm going to take my time with your sister. The little blonde one is to be mine."

Rage threatened to bubble out of me, but I bit my tongue, tasting blood. He wanted to provoke me, wanted me to show him how much his vile words affected me. I. Would. Not. Give. In.

Instead, I smiled up at him. "I've seen your death, Darren Radnor. And it's going to be glorious."

The King snarled, fear clouding his gaze, and slapped me across the face, knocking me to the side. "Little bitch." He turned to the other Kings. "Can we wait for the next full moon? This one needs to be properly broken in."

"No, Darren," the King at the top of the circle snapped. "It must be tonight."

A third King stepped forward, his face cloaked in shadow, but I could feel his poisonous smile when he spoke. "I have another idea."

"Make it quick, Samuel." The King who appeared to be in charge snapped at this one, too.

The creepy one slipped behind me, and I resisted the urge to shiver in revulsion when his fingers danced down my spine. "Let your wings out, lumen princess."

*No.* I shook my head slightly in refusal.

The creeper pressed his hands to my back, and I nearly cried out. It felt like needles digging into my skin as he whispered words beneath his breath. There was nothing I could do in this moment to stop him, and my wings wooshed out. At least they knocked the creep in the face.

My moment of satisfaction quickly died when the foul King grabbed my left wing and held it wide. Bile rose once more at the inappropriate touch. Our wings were sacred, meant only to be embraced by our mates. Before I could even blink, the big one was there, sawing my wing in jagged cuts. The scream I uttered was like nothing I'd ever heard from myself. The pain was excruciating. I coughed and sputtered as my voice gave out completely. When they started on the second wing, my voice was gone, and the croaks of agony leaving my being were hideous and humiliating. The Kings laughed as I writhed, chained to the floor.

Blood poured from the wounds, and the four Kings moved as one, dipping their fingers in my blood and drawing a star on the floor, with me at the center. Darren dug his fingers into the wound, and I groaned in pain.

"Fuck, that sound is delicious. I want to paint my cock in your blood before I fuck you with it." Darren's cruel voice was miles away.

Or at least, it felt far away. My mind was beginning to shut down, protecting me from the pain.

When the bloody star was completed, the candles sprang to life, and I felt my power seeping out of me and into their spell.

They chanted faster, eager for my death and their own rise to power. But greed would be their downfall. I lifted my tongue and plucked the small stone from my mouth. My mother gave it to me before I was brought here, and I knew what I needed to do next. With every single ounce of my strength, and every shining piece of my soul, I surrendered my magic to the stone. It was called luxenite, and this particularly rare stone was the only one of its kind with the power to hold a lumen's soul, the source of our Vis-El.

The crux of it was, when a lumen chose to do this, their soul was lost to the endless darkness, unable to rest among our ancestors amidst the stars. But it was worth it. I sent my heart away to Nuri, begging her forgiveness, for I would not meet her in the next life. And yet, it was the only way. The only way for my sisters to win this war. Michaela would need my power. With this sacrifice, I could save them all.

The chanting cult members carried on, but I was strong enough to resist, I would be strong enough for this. One of the Kings shouted angrily, realizing something wasn't working. The power drained from me, but not to them, into the stone.

Movement to my right nearly broke my concentration, but I didn't look away. I knew who had come.

"How the hell did she get out?" The creepy king shouted. "Seize her at once!"

But these fools could not contain Aurora Valdis. In the next moment, her voice rang out, power spilling from her in waves. Her words grew louder, the light emanating from her blinding to the humans. Several screamed in agony, and their deaths fueled me. I chanted the final words of my own incantation, feeling the last of my Vis-El slip away into the stone. It was gone. I was mortal.

"You did well, my angel." My mother's soft voice was suddenly close. "My brave, beautiful daughter. I love you. You will find peace."

Her voice soothed my aching body. The tip of her finger touched my temple, and I moaned as a spark of power seeped beneath my skin, setting the delicate beam of purest magic alight within my soul. Tears sprang from my eyes as I slumped to the side, unable to thank her for this gift, or tell her one last time how much I truly loved her. The final words of Aurora Valdis had passed. A sonic boom echoed in the room, knocking out everyone within the walls of the manor. Utter silence descended.

My mother, the most powerful creature I'd ever known, was gone. She didn't tell me all, though. She hadn't said her final act would be to save my soul and see hers lost. For there was only one other way to gift a mortal the chance to live on among the stars. The last ember of her power went into me.

The silence was deafening, enough so that the soft footsteps of someone approaching echoed like a drum. He knelt beside me. Ezekiel. It took all my strength to open my enclosed fist and present the stone.

"For Michaela." The words croaked out of me, and I could only hope he understood. That he was truly trustworthy in this task. I'd seen it briefly, the love he had for his son would ensure his loyalty.

He nodded, bright eyes filled with devastating sadness. "It shall be done. Rest now, brave child," he murmured, his voice so unlike the others. The voice of a father who loved his children.

Nothing else needed to be said. And in the next moment, he was gone.

# CHAPTER FOURTEEN

## Nuriela

Her screams tore through my soul. When the chanting stopped, when Aurora's final act was completed, I ran to my mate. Bodies littered the floor. Not all dead, most only knocked out. The Kings would have ensured their safety. We weren't that lucky. Four young boys, no more than my own age, also lay among the bodies. Aurora called them the Princes. My brain barely registered the one prince looked like the boy from the carnival. She also said they weren't to be harmed.

Lucky for all of them, my focus was only on one broken body on the floor. My knees hit the marble hard, but I couldn't feel it. Tears blurred my vision when I took in her beautiful, mutilated wings. Lailah wasn't moving. I lifted her head gently into my lap. The softest groan escaped her bloody lips.

Her eyes didn't open, but the ghost of a smile traced those heart-shaped lips. "Nuri," she whispered, her voice fractured and broken from the screams. "Memento vivre."

Lailah's final breath released from her body, and I shuddered, feeling her soul escape this earthly plane. I titled my head back and screamed my heartbreak into the silence. She was gone.

*Remember to live.*

Lailah's final words reverberated in my head like a death knell. Life was meaningless without her. And she knew I would consider ending it just so I could join her among the stars. But of course, even in death, she was ordering me around. How could I refuse her final order? I pledged my life to hers, and I would not break that oath now.

The sound of footsteps caught my attention, and I whirled around, prepared to kill whomever was still standing. Rage burned within me, and it needed an outlet.

Joseph entered the room, carrying his two daughters. Their bodies were limp in his arms, sleeping heavily, likely given some sedatives to keep them calm. His face was an open wound, tears streaking down his cheeks as he looked on at Aurora and Lailah.

I barely knew the man, but Lailah told me enough about him. He was trustworthy. When his gaze turned to me, he stiffened, arms tightening around his living children.

My wings disappeared, and I raised my arms. "I mean you no harm."

"Who are you?" he asked, his voice gruff with heartache. Blood dripped from a wound on his head.

My own gaze lingered on the broken lumen at the center of the circle. "Hers."

"Nuriela," he murmured, closing his eyes and shaking his head, as if he could shuffle his thoughts into place. "Of course. My mind is…scattered. Her mate."

I huffed a strangled sound, something between a sob and a laugh. "Of course. How Lailah and I ever thought we could hide something from her, I'll never know."

Joseph smiled softly. "Do you want to come with us?"

"No." I shook my head. He didn't need to know my plans, and I needed time to grieve alone.

He nodded, an understanding between us. "This night is only the beginning."

His words rang out in the silent room, and I watched them go without a response. I hugged Lailah's body to my own one last time. I couldn't take her with me. When the Kings awoke and found her body missing, there would be a hunt. So after pressing one last kiss to her lips, I placed her body back where she died. With one final look at my mate, I followed after Joseph.

Joseph piled his daughters into an SUV and fled quickly. The Kings and their lame-ass cult minions would wake soon. I watched them go then followed behind, keeping myself hidden in the clouds.

Lailah said her sisters were the important players of this grand scheme. And only with their help would the war between our people end and this stupid human cult be defeated. A small part of me hated them. Why should they get to live and fight while Lailah died? How was *this* the right way to win?

Aurora's final act officially demolished all connections between Stella Terra and this world, so not only was I unable to go home, but I was stuck living among the foul, idiotic humans who killed my mate.

Joseph Bronwen finally stopped his stolen car outside some tiny, one-stoplight town. It reminded me of one of the outer villages back home. Sometimes we influenced other worlds, like the creation of cities such as New Orleans, and sometimes daemons and lumens copied things from other worlds, like this tiny town. While I hated being stuck here, I was mildly curious to see how the mortals settled their world in real life and not just pictures and stories.

Travelling between worlds was reserved for royalty, or the council members. Lailah begged her mother to let me, but Aurora always said it wasn't my time. I suppose it was now.

Joseph parked in front of a church, and I watched from above as he guided Seraphina inside. They weren't gone long, but only Joseph came back out. He was leaving his daughter? This was not part of the plan, or if it was, no one told me. How could I keep up with both sisters when they were separated?

Joseph sped off into the night, and I decided to stay with the daughter he left behind. Using my power to cloak my footsteps, I crept into the church. Seraphina sat in a pew, quietly sobbing. She wasn't there long before a nun appeared from a door beyond the altar. She rushed to the crying child and quickly ushered her away.

Seraphina was safe for now. Which meant I had time to kill. Starting tonight, I would train every day, analyze the humans. Stalk the cult members. Every secret they tried to keep hidden, I would uncover. I would take everything from them. And only with their deaths would I finally be able to rest.

*My warrior,* the wind whispered, and I could almost smell the lavender oil Lailah always smelled of. I would become her warrior. One who would not have to hide when death arrived, a champion willing to sacrifice everything.

"I will be the warrior you need, Lailah. And I will find you again in the next life," I whispered the oath and leapt into the night sky.

# CHAPTER FIFTEEN

## Nuriela

There was something wrong with Seraphina. She stomped down the street muttering to herself. I must have missed something in the few hours I was gone. Today, I left only because I had a lead on Joseph and Michaela. He was surprisingly good at hiding, and maybe I was mildly impressed. Seraphina was the opposite. She was loud, foul-mouthed, and constantly attracting danger. It was exhausting.

But that voice in my head was murmuring a warning. I closed my eyes and sensed her emotions. They were mostly filled with rage and betrayal. But who betrayed her? The girl was a loner. Dodging foster families and emotional connections to people like it was her damn job. Not that I blamed her. She and I had that in common, at least.

The sun had finally set, and evening carried on while I watched Seraphina tuck a backpack in an alley and set off into the night, heading down a familiar road. She currently lived at a gymnasium. I didn't feel the need to offer her a room at my place. Part of her whole growing up and becoming the woman she needed to be included figuring shit out on her own. Sure, I occasionally left money on the street in front of her or kept the cops from finding her when she stole food and clothing, but that was it. She was on her own. My wings carried me through the clouds, swooping lazily in the sky while she toddled on. Her next stop was curious. Seraphina broke into a mechanic shop. When she exited, she was carrying what appeared to be a full can of gasoline.

I arched an eyebrow. "What are you up to?" I murmured to myself, the breeze carrying the words away into the night.

Seraphina tucked the can of gas into the basket on the front of her bicycle and peddled furiously in the direction of the gymnasium. Well, this was certainly strange, but I wasn't going to intervene. Not yet, anyway.

She rode around to the back of the gym, avoiding the bright lights of the front parking lot and likely the cameras. I noted a single SUV in the parking lot and two pink bicycles parked in the rack out front before swooping down and landing on the room. Using the hatch for roof access, I snuck into the gym to find her. Muffled screams of pure agony reached my ears from the far side of the building where the offices were located.

Keeping to the shadows and using my power to cloak my presence, I crept through the halls, following Seraphina's voice.

"You will never harm another little girl again," she snarled. "And when I find out who the others are, I'll line their dead bodies up right beside yours."

Groans and a rapid heartbeat reached my ears. It appeared she had a man tied up in the office. And he had been hurting young women. Can't say that I disagreed with her threats. The smell of gas reached my nose a few moments before Seraphina appeared in the doorway, a steady stream of gasoline trickling out of the can she stole.

I took off down the hall and away from her line of sight. Seraphina continued to pour the gas over every surface of every office. When she ran out, Seraphina pulled out a set of matches and without even hesitating, lit the match and tossed it to the floor. The building went up in flames instantly. The crazy-ass girl darted out the back door and slumped back on her ass in the empty lot behind the building, watching the flames grow higher and higher. Eventually she stood, grabbed her bicycle, and pedaled away from the building and back to the street. Only this time, she passed the front doors and paused at the bike rack.

"No!" she shouted, running toward the burning building. But it was too late. The entire damn place was on fire.

Sirens blared in the distance, and with a cry of frustration, she took off into the night. Beneath all the noise of the roaring fire and the incoming fire trucks, the softest cries reached my heightened senses. I leapt into action, tucking my wings in and using my power of air to snuff out the fire as I dove into a window.

"Where are you?!" I shouted into the flames.

Soft cries for help came from the direction of the main gym. I dissolved my wings and ran through the flames, using a shield of air to keep the fire at bay. The building was collapsing around me, and I urged my body to move faster.

No more cries reached my ears, but I could hear their hearts still beating. One was faint, nearly gone, and the other not far behind. I raced through the burning building and found the two girls passed out in the center of the gym. Debris blocked their way out in every direction; they didn't stand a chance.

Flames licked at the leggings of the older girl, and she began to scream. I blasted away the debris and ran at them, snuffing out the fire burning the girl. The scent of burned flesh filled the air. I scooped her into my arms, and she groaned in pain. There wasn't time to stick around, and I couldn't carry them both. My ears couldn't detect a heartbeat in the smaller child. She was already gone.

With a snarl of determination, I jumped into the air, my wings snapping out, and rushed directly at the ceiling. I aimed my body for one of the skylights, blasting the glass away and shielding the girl in my arms.

Fire followed us out into the night, the flames growing ever higher. Fire trucks had arrived and worked to put out the flames as we took off into the night. I flew directly to a hospital, uncertain how I could help the girl. She was human. Using too much Vis-El on a human was dangerous. They could go mad, their little bodies unable to handle the power.

So I dropped her into the emergency room, shouting for help before I ran out. I flicked my wrists at the security cameras, altering the footage enough to keep me out of it.

The nurses and doctors sprang into action, quickly admitting the girl and doing whatever it was they did to save her life. Something about the girl tugged at my soul. She seemed close to Seraphina's age, maybe a year younger. And this little feeling in the back of my mind told me I should stay and wait for her. So I did.

It wasn't long before the girl was carted to her own room. Luckily, it had a window. I swooped down and flicked the lock, opening it and landing lightly beside her bed. She was bandaged up almost entirely. The fire had burned her from ankle to neck down her left side.

She was sleeping, a morphine drip tucked in her vein on the undamaged arm. I sat beside her and held my hand out over her body. Heat from the fire lingered. Closing my eyes, I scanned her form for the worst of the damage and whispered quietly, offering what little bit of healing I could without doing any further damage to her psyche.

The girl stirred as I finished. Her eyelids fluttered open, and bright, emerald-green eyes met mine. They were filled with pain, fear and anger. Not unlike my own.

"Who are you?" She coughed out the words.

"Someone who can help," I murmured, reaching out a hand and pressing down gently on her throat. She didn't move, only watched. Closing my eyes once more, I sought out the smoke in her lungs and forced it up out of her body.

She coughed heavily then sucked in a fresh breath of oxygen. "Thank you."

I nodded, not really wanting her thanks.

"My sister?" she whispered, and our eyes locked once more. But I didn't need to speak for her to know her sister was dead.

She didn't cry, but closed her eyes and bit down on her lip, retreating within herself. Like me, she was alone. And in that moment, I knew this resilient being was the one I was meant to find.

"Lo?" I spoke the name softly and her eyes snapped open.

"Do I know you?" Her voice quivered.

I shook my head. "No. But I think we were meant to find each other. I cannot take away all your scars, but I can help you get revenge."

Lo's eyes sparked with fury. "She did this. She killed my sister. I heard Sara's voice. And my father's."

This was going to be difficult, but only with the complete truth could she handle the future I had to offer. While she recovered, I was able to find information via the police. Human minds were quite malleable. And in doing so, understood why Seraphina started that fire.

"Your father was a pedophile." The statement didn't surprise her. "He was going to offer your sister to someone tonight. Instead, he died in that fire."

"So did my sister," Lo snapped, her body shaking with anger, and something else. I sensed guilt.

"I don't believe Sara would have set that fire if she knew you were there." This was true. Seraphina might be a general nuisance, but she wasn't evil. If anything, she offered help to those who needed it. "Why were you there tonight?"

Lo closed her eyes and her lip quivered. "We were supposed to be. My father said I had to bring Maddie and get to the gym. He said he had a present for her."

Fucking men. How could a father do such a thing to his own child? I nodded. "Did he…did it happen to you, too?"

Lo shook her head. "Almost. Once, I think. But the memory is vague. I was maybe four years old. My mother was still alive then. I think she stopped it. Then she died giving birth to my sister a few years later."

Her story was tragic, and the memories of my own losses threatened to spill out. I stood, shoving them back into the corners of my mind. "If you wish to go your own way now, I will leave you. But on the chance that what you seek is revenge, I can help with that."

Lo's emerald eyes regarded mine for some time before she spoke. "I want revenge."

I nodded grimly. "This path is dangerous and you will learn of monsters far greater than your father. I can't promise you'll survive this war."

Lo shrugged then winced at the movement. "I don't have anything else left."

She was alone in this world. Lost and set adrift, as I was. Perhaps together, we could heal some parts of us. Or at the very least, give her something to live for.

"My name is Nuriela." I stood at my full height and let my wings slowly unfurl at my back. "And here is where your path for vengeance begins."

THE END

# EPILOGUE

## Leona

Sweat coated my skin, and fire licked up my spine. The flames were everywhere. They burned me, marked me.

"No!" I screamed, sitting up in bed. Dreams of fire were my constant companion. Less so when Nuriela was nearby, but even she could not always keep them away.

A soft breeze blew in from the window of my room. Or rather, the room I occupied at Vespertine Hall. We were staying here while Seraphina and Michaela learned to control their powers. So far, they were mildly successful. It was difficult to watch Seraphina train with fire. I know it wasn't her fault my sister died, it was mine, too. My father's and hers. And most of all, mine. If only I had accepted the monster within him sooner, maybe I could have protected us. Found a way out. At the very least, killed him myself.

I crawled out of the too-soft bed and poured a glass of water, swallowing it down in three gulps. Fine, it wasn't too soft. It was all just too much. This place was practically a palace. Although Nuriela said it had nothing on the palace in Caelum. And I was eager to see it. And maybe find a little magic of my own. If the creepy cult guys could gain access to magic, so could I.

Nuriela said it was dangerous for a human, that I could even go mad, but wasn't I already?

Not that she had any idea. But the dreams certainly implied my brain was finally cracked. The dreams of the fire were normal, a constant companion. But not him. He was something new, something more. When I dreamed of him. It didn't truly feel like dreaming. It was more like…another reality. He called my name in the darkest parts of my dreams. Seduced me with promises of a future where I was powerful, feared. I was no longer the weak link of the group.

Yes, Nuriela taught me to fight, and sure, I was really fucking good at it. But when a daemon launched a fireball at your head, a badass roundhouse kick was pretty useless.

"Get over yourself, Lo," I grumbled, flopping back into bed. "You're just a human. A scarred, broken human."

And no one wants one of those. The thought formed in my mind as I drifted back to sleep.

*I do.*
*You're here.*
*Always.*
*Where do you go when I wake up?*
*I slumber. Deep beneath the castle. Waiting.*
*What are you waiting for?*
*You.*
*Why me? What am I?*
*My salvation.*

The voice in my dreams was deep and laced with dangerous promises. I was his salvation. The prince to his sleeping beauty, it would seem. But who was he and how did I find him? Not even Nuriela knew about my dreams. I was afraid she would take them away. Some part of me knew this monster was just that, a monster. He wanted *me*, and feeling wanted by a monster was a high unlike any other.

So I would keep him a secret, at least for now.

I tossed in the bed, blood rushing to my core as his voice filled my mind. My hand slipped below the sheets and under my silk panties. They were soaked. For him. His voice was enough to bring my body to ruin.

*Let your body lead you to me.*
*How?*
*Can't you feel it?*
*What?*
*Lust. Desire. Sin.*

I pumped two fingers inside my pussy and moaned. My mind was half in dreamland, half awake.

*I want to feel you.*
*Soon. My little beauty. Soon.*

My fingers teased and pleasured my clit, and when the monster growled within the dark recesses of my mind, I cried out, the orgasm rushing through me. Lust saturated my blood, and I moaned, feeling the wetness leak from me. But it was never enough.

I would find this monster of mine, and when I did, I would unleash him.

# ABOUT THE AUTHOR

S. D. Paine is a writer of fantasy and romance of the dark and paranormal variety. She loves a good plot twist and creating morally gray characters. She reads constantly, and cannot function without at least two cups of coffee. Stephanie lives in the Midwest with her family and a small horde of adopted dogs and a crazy cat.

www.sdpaineauthor.com

Follow the author on Facebook, Instagram and TikTok at @everafterauthor.

# ACKNOWLEDGEMENTS

I would like to thank my amazing editor, Andrea, and my PAs, Nicole and Holly, for their constant encouragement, creative input and general organization of my messiness to help bring these books to life. Love you all so much! And a massive thank you to my Street Team and ARC readers. Your comments, reviews and social media posts give me all the feels. Amy, I adore you and LOVE how you brought the world to life with the map!

The bookish community has been amazing, and I've found kick-ass friends among the readers and fellow indie authors. I know social media has its highs and lows, but without it, I wouldn't have met some of the people I would now consider friends.

And finally thank you to my friends and family. Marissa and Bri for being the best alphas/betas/arcs/listening-to-me-constantly-talk-about-the-story besties. And my core friend group, love you all for supporting me and my books!! And fam, I'm really shocked you're reading this spicy series. Please don't tell me what you think about it. *wink*